big & SMALL

Original Korean text by Mi-ae Lee
Illustrations by Soo-ji Park
Korean edition © Aram Publishing

This English edition published by big & SMALL in 2016
by arrangement with Aram Publishing
English text edited by Joy Cowley
English edition © big & SMALL 2016

Distributed in the United States and Canada by
Lerner Publishing Group, Inc.
241 First Avenue North
Minneapolis, MN 55401 U.S.A.
www.lernerbooks.com
ISBN: 978-1-925186-59-8
Printed in Korea

Wheels Go Round and Round

Written by Mi-ae Lee
Illustrated by Soo-ji Park
Edited by Joy Cowley

Big wheels and little wheels
traveled around the world.
They came to a country
where there were no wheels.

People struggled to move their things in boxes.

A wheel rolled up to them. It asked, "Why don't you use wheels?"

Now people pull a wheeled wagon.
Wheels make it easy to move heavy loads.
Round wheels roll well on the ground.

The day was hot and the road was long.
People felt very tired.

A wheel bounced up to them.
"Wait!" it said. "You can use wheels!"

Now the people drive
in cars with four wheels.
"We can travel a long way.
We don't get tired,
thanks to wheels."

The woman was angry.
"This vacuum cleaner
is too heavy!" she said.

Along came a little wheel.
"You need wheels," it said.

Now the woman likes cleaning the floor. "It's so easy," she says. "The vacuum rolls across the rug. Thanks to wheels!"

Mothers tried to hold their babies.
They cried. It was noisy!
What a fuss!

A wheel rolled up. It said,
"You can use wheels!"

Now the happy mothers take their babies for walks in strollers. They say, "This is so much better, thanks to wheels."

The wheels were feeling very happy.
"Everybody is thanking us!"
They rode very fast on the skateboard.

Oops!
They fell off and went spinning
in all directions.

Things with wheels can go fast!
We should be very careful
with them.

How Were Wheels Invented?

Today we use wheels on many moving things.
How and when were wheels invented?

The first wheels were logs,
round trunks or branches of trees.
Blocks of stone rolled on top
of the logs. Canoes slid into
the water on logs.

In ancient times there were
no wheels. People had to
carry heavy things. They
shared the load with others.
They carried the animals
they hunted on their backs.

The next big discovery was the axle.
It went through a center hole
in a round slice of a tree trunk.
People made wheeled wagons.

The wheels we have today
turn on a central axle.

I Want to Know about Wheels

I have the smallest area that touches the floor.

Why are wheels round?

It is because objects that are round roll well. A round object has a small area that touches the ground. It rolls easily when it is pushed or pulled.

Do all wheels carry loads?

No. Wheels are used as gears in clocks and other machines. Wheels also turn other wheels. They connect with belts or chains.

Why are car tires black?

Tires are made of rubber and filled with air. This helps lessen rattles and bumps on the road. It gives passengers a smooth ride. Tires are mixed with a black powder made from carbon. The powder makes tires strong and durable. It is what makes car tires black.

When was the first car invented?

Flemish inventor Ferdinand Verbiest built a tiny car powered by steam in 1672. It was just a toy, but it moved by itself and may have been the world's first car. Karl Benz invented the first modern car in 1886.

Wheels Go Round and Round

In a land without wheels, work is hard. It is hard to carry things. It is hard to pull things. The people get tired walking too. But wheels come to town and make everything easier. They let carts roll. Cars and machines use them too. The wheels make it easy to work.
All the people thank the wheels for their help.

Let's think!

Why are wheels round?

How do wheels move on the ground?

Why is work easier with wheels?

What ways do you use wheels?

Let's do!

See how much faster wheels make you go.
Try walking from one spot to another.
Use a watch to track how long it takes.
Then ride on a skateboard or bicycle.
Go the same distance. Ask a friend to time you.
Were you faster with wheels?